This Book Belongs To:

_____

To my little mice,
Sóley and Salka,
quiet and loud but,
most importantly,
always together as sisters

This paperback edition first published in 2017 by Andersen Press Ltd.,
20 Vauxhall Bridge Road, London SW1V 2SA.

First published in 2017 by Alfred A. Knopf,
an imprint of Random House Children's Books,
a division of Penguin Random House LLC, New York.

Printed and bound in Malaysia.

10 9 8 7 6 5 4 3 2 1

British Library Cataloging in Publication Data available.

ISBN 978 1 78344 512 7

Birgitta Sif

SWISH & SQUEAK'S
Noisy Day

Andersen Press

In the early morning, it's still too
dark to see, but Swish hears the ticking
of the clock and the birds
in the trees.

Wait... what is it that her ears hear?
Is it a crocodile chomping the
kitchen table into tiny pieces?

CRUNCH

CRUNCH

CRUNCH CRUNCH

CRUNCH

CRUNCH

Swooshhhh
swooooshh
swoosh

Swish hears the swoosh
of her toothbrush...

nibble
nibble

and a tiny nibble as she
packs their lunches.

Mwuaahhh
mwuah Mwuahhh

Her ears hear kisses goodbye –
and one extra, saved safe in her pocket.

Squeeeakkk

squeak squeak

Swish hears the squeaky
waggon wheel...

Oh, wait! And... what is it
that her ears hear *now*?

STOMP
STOMP
STOMP

Oh, it's just an elephant trampling
down the stairs. She should have known!

"C'mon, Squeak.
It's time to go!"

On the way to school, her ears hear
a racecar driver trying to speed past.

VROOM VROOM
beep beep
toot toot

Then she hears that they're late!
Better run...

eeeek

Swish hears her heart beating fast as she listens and learns to be brave!

munch munch

She hears stomachs growling just before lunch!

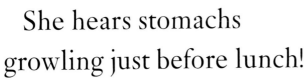

Squeeeak

tooot

And she hears the school band, very, very out of tune!

pum pum

bah ba

Her ears hear

A LOT!

At the end of the day,
their eyes can't find each other...

but their ears can.

On their way home, they stop by
Swish's favourite peaceful place...
and she hears the perfect quiet.

Lalalalalalala
Lalalalalalala

(Or at least she tries to...)

And when bedtime arrives, she hears the sound of just ONE more adventure before the lights go out.

But in the dark,
her ears hear a soft whisper from Squeak.

"I'm scared."

So she sings their song.

Then all is still... night must be here.

But wait... what is it that her ears hear?

zzz-Zzzz-ZZzzz-hngGGggh-PpbhwzZZ

zzz-ZZzzz-hngGGggh-PpbhwzZZ-zzzZZ

zzz-ZZzzz-hngGGggh

PpbhwzZZ-zzzZZ

Shhhhh... it's the sound of a little mouse dreaming.